Danny's Smelly Toothbrush

BRIANÓG BRADY DAWSON

• Pictures by Michael Connor •

THE O'BRIEN PRESS
DUBLIN

First published 1999 by The O'Brien Press Ltd.,
20 Victoria Road, Dublin 6, Ireland
Tel. +353 1 4923333 Fax. +353 1 4922777
e-mail books@obrien.ie
Web www.obrien.ie
Reprinted 2000

ISBN: 0-86278-611-8

2   3   4   5   6   7   8   9   10
00   01   02   03   04   05   06

British Library Cataloguing-in-publication Data
Dawson, Brianóg Brady
Danny's smelly toothbrush. - (O'Brien pandas ; bk. 11)
1.Teeth - Care and hygiene - Juvenile fiction
2.Children's stories
I.Title
823.9'14[J]

The O'Brien Press receives
assistance from

The Arts Council
An Chomhairle Ealaíon

Typesetting, layout, editing: The O'Brien Press Ltd.
Cover separations: C&A Print Services Ltd., Dublin
Printing: Cox & Wyman Ltd., Britain.

Can YOU spot the panda
hidden in the story?

Danny Brown looked
at his toothbrush.
The bristles were bent
and twisted.
'That brush is no good
anymore,' said Mum.
'Put it in the bin.'

Danny was delighted.
He **hated** brushing his teeth.

'My teeth are
never dirty,' Danny said.
'I always lick them clean.'

Later, Granny came to visit.
She smiled at Danny.
'Look what I've got for you,'
she said.

Granny opened her bag.
She took out a bright, new,
shiny, yellow toothbrush.

Danny was not pleased.
I'm going to get rid
of this toothbrush,
he thought.

But he smiled sweetly.
'Thanks, Granny,' he said.
'It's so shiny!
I'll take it upstairs right now.'

Danny went upstairs.

He hated his new toothbrush.

He hit the handle on the stairs.

He hit it very hard.

But the handle didn't break.

'Hey you, Hairy Face!'
said Danny.
'I'm going to destroy you.'

Suddenly Danny had a
wonderful idea.
'The loo,' he said.
'I'll flush it down the loo.'

He dashed into the bathroom.
He looked at his
new toothbrush.
'You're dead!' he said.
Danny smiled.
Then he lifted
the toilet lid.

Plop!

The shiny, new toothbrush
fell into the water
with a tiny splash.

Danny closed the lid.

He flushed the toilet.

'Goodbye forever, toothbrush,'
he sang.

He grinned at himself
in the bathroom mirror.
Then, slowly,
he lifted the toilet lid.
He peeped inside.

The new toothbrush was
still there!
It was bobbing about
on top of the water.

'Danny!' Mum was
coming up the stairs.
'Mark and Darren are here.
Time to play!'

'Oh no!' said Danny.
'What do I do now?'

Danny rolled up his sleeve.

He reached into the toilet.

He fished out his
shiny new toothbrush.

'**Yuck**,' he said.

Danny ran downstairs.
He could feel the wet
toothbrush in his pocket.
'Hi, Mark. Hi, Darren,' he said.
'Let's go to the park.'

Then Danny called his dog.
'Come on, Keeno,' he said.
Keeno licked Danny's face –
big wet licks.
'**Yuck**!' said Danny.

Danny and the boys set off.
'Guess what!' said Danny
to his friends.
'I need your help.
I have to **get rid of**
something.'

Darren was excited.
'Sure,' he said.
'What is it?'

'Granny got me
a new toothbrush!' said Danny.
'Mum told her to.
Mum's crazy about
brushing teeth.
I have to do it
every morning
and **every night**.
I'm sick of it!'

Danny took the toothbrush
from his pocket.
'**I hate it**!' he said.

'It's a monster!' said Mark.

The three boys ran
all the way to the park.
Keeno ran with them.

Then Danny had an idea.
Danny threw his toothbrush
as far as he could.
'Fetch, Keeno. Fetch!' he yelled.

Keeno ran off.
Soon he was back.
He had the toothbrush
in his mouth.
It was wet all over.

Danny, Mark and Darren
had lots of fun with
Keeno and the toothbrush.

Then they got tired.

They sat down.

'Hey!' said Danny.

'Smell my toothbrush now!'

The boys smelled
Danny's brush.
'Yuck!' said Mark.
'Wicked!' said Darren.
He held his nose.
He pretended to faint.
Danny and Mark laughed.

Then Danny had another idea.
'Keeno needs
his hair brushed,' he said.
'Let's use my toothbrush.'

The boys took turns
brushing Keeno's hair with
Danny's new toothbrush!
Soon it was full of dog hair.
'It smells worse now!'
said Mark.

'That's because Keeno
needs a bath!' said Danny.
'Let's go to the pond.'

The pond looked very green.

'This water is filthy!'
said Danny. 'Let's dip
my toothbrush in.'
He dipped his toothbrush
in the pond.
Soon it was covered
in green scum.
'It's the Wicked Pond Monster!'
said Darren.

Danny was having
a great time.
Getting rid of his toothbrush
was **fun**.

Suddenly, Mark saw
someone coming.
'Quick!' he said.
'It's Conor Daly!'
Danny and his friends
turned to go.
Nobody liked the school bully.

But Conor Daly saw them.
'What have you got there,
Danny?' he said.

Conor grabbed the toothbrush.
He laughed.
'That's a lovely toothbrush,
Danny Brown!' he said.
'Did it fall in the pond?'

Danny reached
for the toothbrush.

But Conor gave him a push.
'Not so fast!' he said.
'There's something nasty
on my shoe.'

Then Conor Daly
cleaned his shoe
with Danny's new toothbrush.

He laughed loudly.
Then he threw the toothbrush
at Danny and ran off.

But Danny was thrilled.
Conor Daly had made a mess
of his new toothbrush –
forever!

Danny picked up
the new toothbrush.
It looked awful.
It felt awful.
It smelled awful.
'What do we do now?'
asked Mark.

'This toothbrush is dead!'
said Danny.
'We'll have to bury it!'

Danny, Mark and Darren
began to dig a hole.

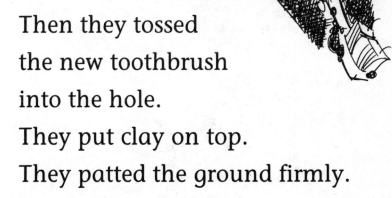

Then they tossed
the new toothbrush
into the hole.
They put clay on top.
They patted the ground firmly.

'**Gone forever**!'

said Danny.

He danced on the clay.

Darren and Mark danced

on it too.

'We have destroyed
the wicked toothbrush!'
shouted Darren.
The three boys cheered.

Danny was delighted.

'It's gone!' he cried.

'**Gone**. **Gone**. **Gone**.'

Danny would never see
his new toothbrush
again.

'Hello, boys,' called a voice.
Danny looked around.
It was Mum and
Danny's little sister, Susie.

'Just in time!' said Danny
to his friends.

'We've brought a little picnic,'
said Mum. 'Who's hungry?'
'Me! Me! Me!' yelled Danny,
Mark and Darren together.
They all sat down on the grass.

Susie began to crawl.
'Go and explore, Susie,'
said Mum.

'Yes, Susie, give us some peace,'
said Danny.
The boys laughed.

After a while, Mum looked up.

'Susie is digging again,'
she said.

'Susie loves digging.'

Soon Susie came back.
She had something
in her mouth.

Danny couldn't believe his eyes.
'Oh no!' he cried.
'It's my **new toothbrush**!'

Mum took the toothbrush.

'Oh dear!' she cried.

'Your lovely new toothbrush,
Danny! Were you showing it
to your friends?'

Danny looked at
the toothbrush.
He was in trouble now!
He felt sick.

But Mum said: 'Don't worry.
I'll clean it. I've got
a special cleaner.
You'll be able to use it tonight,
Danny! I promise.'

Danny thought of
Conor Daly's dirty shoe.

He thought of
Keeno's dribbles.

He thought of the
dirty pond.

He thought of
Susie's digging.

And then Danny thought of ...
THE LOO!

Danny fell back on the grass.
'I'll never do anything
like this again,' he said.
'Never. Never. Never.'

But I think he will, don't you?
Danny's just that kind of kid.

Well, did you find him?